One cold winter morning, Jon was on his way to school when he saw an old lady sitting by the side of the lane.

“Good morning,” he greeted her. “Are you all right? It is a very cold morning to be sitting here.”

“I am hoping to find something to eat,” the old lady replied.

Jon's family were quite poor, so he only had a slice of bread that his mother had given him for his lunch. However, he took the slice of bread out of his bag and gave it to the old lady.

“Thank you,” she said, “you are very kind.”

Later that afternoon, as Jon made his way home, he saw the old lady again standing by the side of the lane. She was holding a little black cooking pot.

"Hello," she said. "Because you were so kind to me this morning, I have a present for you."

"This is a magic porridge pot. All you have to do is tap the side and say 'Cook porridge pot, cook!' When you want it to stop, you tap it twice and say 'Stop porridge pot, stop!'"

Jon thanked the old lady, took the porridge pot, and hurried home to try it out.

His mother and brother looked at the battered pot and said, “What have you found? Why have you picked up that dirty old pot?”

“An old lady gave it to me,” replied Jon. “I gave her my lunch because she was hungry. She says it is a magic pot.”

"Don't be silly," grumbled his mother. "Of course it isn't a magic pot."

Jon tapped the side of the pot and said, "Cook porridge pot, cook!"

Soon, they could smell porridge, and the little pot quickly filled up with lovely porridge. "Stop porridge pot, stop!" said Jon, tapping it twice.

His mother and brother were amazed. They got a dish each and filled it with the porridge.

“That is a magic pot indeed,” agreed his mother.

“We will never be hungry again” she said happily.

Each morning Jon, his mother, and little brother Fritz had a huge bowl of porridge for breakfast. In the summer, they would add berries and in the winter they would add jam.

Being a generous family, they would sometimes invite others for breakfast or take a bowl of porridge to someone who was ill.

One morning, after Jon had set off for school, his mother went out to the edge of the forest to collect firewood. She left his little brother Fritz in the cottage and told him to be good.

After a while Fritz was bored and decided he was hungry. He looked at the porridge pot and smiled. Then he fetched his bowl and spoon. He stretched up, tapped the pot, and said, "Cook porridge pot, cook!"

The pot started to fill with porridge.

He filled his bowl with porridge and went outside to eat it and to wait for his mother. He completely forgot that he hadn't told the pot to stop cooking. He sat on the bench by the door eating his porridge and didn't notice that the cottage was filling up with porridge.

The porridge bubbled out of the pot, across the floor and then began trickling out into the garden. Fritz's feet were soon covered in porridge, so he stood on the bench. Soon the porridge began to ooze over the top of the bench.

"Help!" cried Fritz in alarm.

His mother came rushing back but there was so much porridge she couldn't get to the cottage or to Fritz. Fritz and his mother were swept away, down the lane to the village, bobbing about in a huge tidal wave of porridge.

When the tide of porridge reached the village school, all of the children rushed out to see the astonishing sight. They could see heads, as well as cats and dogs, and tables and benches all being swept along in the stream of porridge.

Jon ran as quickly as he could around the edge of the village and the river of porridge to his home. He climbed in the back window and swam his way to the pot. He managed to tap the pot twice while yelling out, “Stop porridge pot, stop!”

Once the pot had stopped cooking, and the waves of porridge stopped, everyone struggled free and began to clean up. Porridge was scooped up into all sorts of pots and pans and containers. Cottages, clothes, and children all had to be scrubbed.

But no one in the village was hungry that night, or short of porridge for quite some time!